Ladybird Readers

Scuderia Ferrari: Famous Races

Series Editor: Sorrel Pitts
Written by Nick Coates
Activities written by Catrin Morris

LADYBIRD BOOKS

UK | USA | Canada | Ireland | Australia
India | New Zealand | South Africa

Ladybird Books is part of the Penguin Random House group of companies
whose addresses can be found at global.penguinrandomhouse.com.
www.penguin.co.uk   www.puffin.co.uk   www.ladybird.co.uk

First published 2020
001

Published by arrangement with Franco Cosimo Panini Editore Spa, Modena, Italy
www.paniniragazzi.it

Printed in China

A CIP catalogue record for this book is available from the British Library

ISBN: 978-0-241-40179-8

All correspondence to:
Ladybird Books
Penguin Random House Children's
80 Strand, London WC2R 0RL

Ladybird Readers

Scuderia Ferrari: Famous Races

 To download full story audio in both British and American accents, and to complete
the listening activities at the back of the book, visit **www.ladybirdeducation.co.uk**

Contents

Characters

Enzo Ferrari

José Froilán
González

Niki Lauda

Clay Regazzoni

Gilles
Villeneuve

Michael
Schumacher

Jean Todt

Kimi Räikkönen

CHAPTER ONE

Mille Miglia 1948: The first victory

Scuderia Ferrari is one of the great names in **motor racing***—perhaps the greatest! The Ferrari name comes from the man who started it all—Enzo Anselmo Ferrari.

Enzo as a young man

*Definitions of words in **bold** can be found in the glossary on pages 63-64.

Enzo Ferrari was born in Modena, Italy, in 1898. He always loved cars, and from the age of ten he wanted to be a racing driver.

Enzo as a boy

In 1920, Enzo began to drive for the Alfa Romeo racing team, but in 1929 he started his own team called Scuderia Ferrari.

Enzo in an Alfa Romeo car

At first, Scuderia Ferrari drove Alfa Romeo cars, but in 1939 Enzo started making Ferrari cars, too.

The Ferrari 125 S—the first racing car with the Ferrari name

The first of Scuderia Ferrari's many **victories** came in the Mille Miglia race.

The Mille Miglia was a road race that started at different places in Italy each year.

In 1948, the race was 1,830 kilometers from Brescia to Rome and back.

Clemente Biondetti

On May 2nd and 3rd, Clemente Biondetti and Giuseppe Navone drove their Ferrari 166 S Coupe to win it in 15 hours, 5 minutes and 44 seconds.

The winning Ferrari

CHAPTER TWO
Silverstone 1951: Success in Formula 1

The next great victory for Scuderia Ferrari
was in a **Formula 1 Grand Prix**—the
biggest and most exciting car race in
the world.

It happened on July 14th 1951 at the Grand Prix at Silverstone in the UK. There were twenty cars in the race, and three of them were Ferraris.

Juan Manuel Fangio was the favorite to win. The Alfa Romeo driver was the best in the world—he was the winner of five **Drivers' World Championships**!

The race began. Fangio was soon in front, but close behind was José Froilán González's Ferrari car.

González in his Ferrari 375

As they got near the end of the race, González was able to pass Fangio—and he won by 50 seconds.

Scuderia Ferrari had their first **success** in Formula 1!

CHAPTER THREE

Daytona 1967: On top in the USA

The 24 Hours of Daytona race in the USA is different because two drivers in one car race for 24 hours . . . and in 1967 it was an **amazing** race!

The Ferrari 330 P4

The American Ford team really wanted
to win. They entered six cars and had
200 people to work on them. Scuderia Ferrari
only had three cars and twenty-five people.

However, Scuderia Ferrari had the amazing
330 P4 cars, and one of them was driven by
Lorenzo Bandini and Chris Amon.

Bandini
and Amon

As the hours passed, the Fords stopped one after the other, but the three Ferrari cars drove and drove.

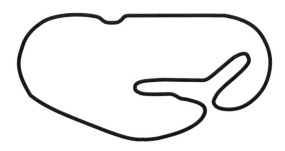

The 24 Hours of Daytona racetrack

After a drive of 4,083 kilometers, Bandini and Amon won. The other two Ferrari cars came second and third, so they drove around the **racetrack** together to **celebrate** Ferrari's amazing victory.

Ferrari came first, second, and third
in the Daytona race!

CHAPTER FOUR

Monza 1975: A double victory in Italy

The 1975 Italian Grand Prix at Monza was another big race for Scuderia Ferrari.

Ferrari hoped to win the **Constructors' Championship**, and their top driver, Niki Lauda, wanted to win the Drivers' World Championship.

Niki Lauda and Clay Regazzoni

It was Scuderia Ferrari's other driver,
Clay Regazzoni, who had the fastest start
and was in first **place** for the whole race.

Clay Regazzoni leading the race

At **lap** 40, Lauda had a problem with his car, so he **slowed down**.

Regazzoni had no problems and won easily. Lauda was third, which was enough for him to become World **Champion**.

Scuderia Ferrari also won the Constructors' Championship.

Regazzoni and Lauda celebrate

CHAPTER FIVE

Monaco 1981: A victory at Monte Carlo

At the Monaco Grand Prix, the cars race through the streets of the city of Monte Carlo. This is different from a normal racetrack because the cars sometimes have to slow down and turn more often.

Everyone said that the Ferraris couldn't win because they had **turbo** engines. A turbo engine is very good for driving fast but not good for turning slowly.

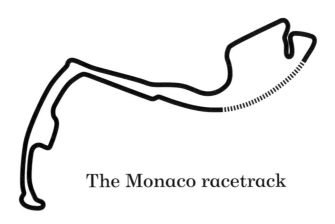

The Monaco racetrack

At first, this was right. Gilles Villeneuve, in the first Ferrari, was a long way behind the leading teams' drivers, Nelson Piquet and Alan Jones. Then, on lap 53 of 76 laps, Piquet drove off the racetrack.

Gilles Villeneuve

Then, Jones had a problem with his car, and he slowed down. On lap 72, Villeneuve passed Jones and won the race.

Everyone was wrong! Villeneuve and Scuderia Ferrari COULD win at Monaco with a turbo engine.

CHAPTER SIX

Imola 1983: A victory for Villeneuve

In May 1983, Scuderia Ferrari raced in the San Marino Grand Prix at the Imola racetrack in Italy.

Scuderia Ferrari had two new drivers,
René Arnoux and Patrick Tambay.

Sadly, Gilles Villeneuve, the great Ferrari
driver from Canada, wasn't with the team
any more. He died in a terrible racing
accident in 1982.

René Arnoux (in car 28) and
Patrick Tambay (in car 27)

The race was a fight between Tambay
and Riccardo Patrese in a Brabham car.
With only five laps to go, Patrese drove off
the racetrack. Tambay won and Arnoux
came third.

Tambay was from France, but at the end of the race he waved the Canadian flag to celebrate and remember Gilles Villeneuve.

Tambay wins for Villeneuve

CHAPTER SEVEN

Monza 1988: Remembering Enzo

On August 14th 1988, Enzo Ferrari died in Italy. He was ninety years old.

The Italian Grand Prix happened a month later at Monza. The Ferrari fans were all there and wanted to remember and celebrate Enzo.

However, Scuderia Ferrari didn't have much hope for the race. At that time, the McLaren team of Alain Prost and Ayrton Senna were winning everything!

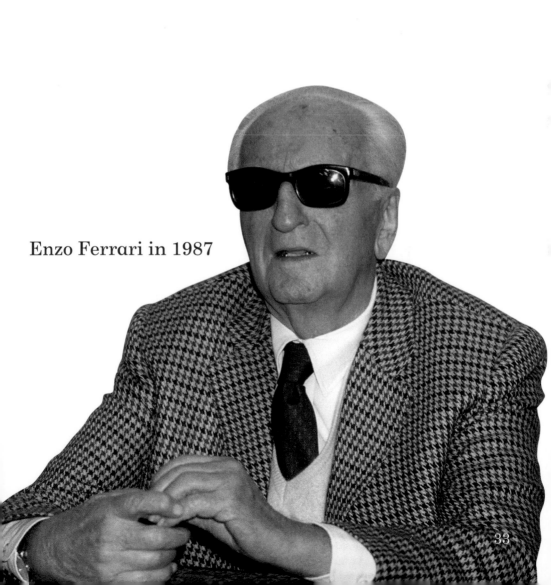

Enzo Ferrari in 1987

At first, the McLarens were in front.
However, in lap 35, Prost's engine suddenly
stopped working. Then, with two laps to
go, Senna's McLaren car hit another car.
He was out of the race!

The two Ferrari drivers, Gerhard Berger and
Michele Alboreto, came first and second.

Ferrari win the race!

Scuderia Ferrari were lucky that day.

The newspapers wrote, "Someone up there loves you, Ferrari!" They were thinking about Enzo Ferrari.

Racing for Enzo Ferrari

CHAPTER EIGHT

Suzuka 2000: Champions after 21 years

In 1979, Jody Scheckter won the Drivers' World Championship in a Ferrari. After that, there was a long wait for Ferrari fans.

But in 2000, a young German driver, Michael Schumacher, was close to changing that for Scuderia Ferrari.

If he won the Japanese Grand Prix at Suzuka, he would be the World Champion.

Michael
Schumacher

The race was amazing! Schumacher started first, but Mika Häkkinen, in a McLaren car, passed him at the first corner. Häkkinen went faster and faster, but Schumacher stayed close behind him.

In lap 37, Häkkinen stopped to get new **tires**. Schumacher drove for another three laps before he changed his tires.

When Schumacher started again, he was in front, but only by 2 seconds.

Schumacher leads after a tire change

When he crossed the finishing line to win, Schumacher cried in his car because he was so excited and happy.

Jean Todt, the General Manager of Scuderia Ferrari, said, "Next time our fans won't have to wait so long."

He was right, because Schumacher won again and again for Scuderia Ferrari.

Schumacher and Häkkinen
at the end of the race

Michael Schumacher—World Champion!

CHAPTER NINE

Suzuka 2003: Schumacher makes it six

Juan Manuel Fangio won five Drivers' World Championships between 1951 and 1957. In 2002, Michael Schumacher won it for the fifth time.

Could he make it six times?

The final Grand Prix of 2003 was at Suzuka, Japan. Schumacher needed to finish in eighth place or higher to win the Championship.

The race at Suzuka, Japan

At first, things didn't go well for Schumacher.
After a small accident in lap 6, he was in
last place.

However, the other Ferrari driver,
Rubens Barrichello, had a good race.
He won, and so Ferrari won the
Constructors' Championship again.

The Ferrari team celebrate their victory

At the same time, Schumacher raced back to finish in eighth place! He did it—he was the first driver to win six World Championships!

**The winner of six
World Championships celebrates**

CHAPTER TEN

Interlagos 2007: The success goes on

When Kimi Räikkönen, driving for Ferrari, started the last race of the year in Brazil, he was in third place in the Drivers' World Championship. He was seven points behind Lewis Hamilton.

To win the Championship, Räikkönen needed to win the race, and Hamilton could not finish in the first six places. Was it possible?

When the race started, Felipe Massa's and Räikkönen's Ferraris raced in front, and Hamilton drove off the racetrack. He started again in last place.

The two Ferraris leading the race

Massa was in front, with Räikkönen just behind him. Then, the two Ferraris quickly changed places, and Räikkönen won!

But where was Hamilton? He only finished in seventh place so Kimi Räikkönen won the Drivers' World Championship!

It was another success for Ferrari in a long line of victories—and there are sure to be many more of them in the future!

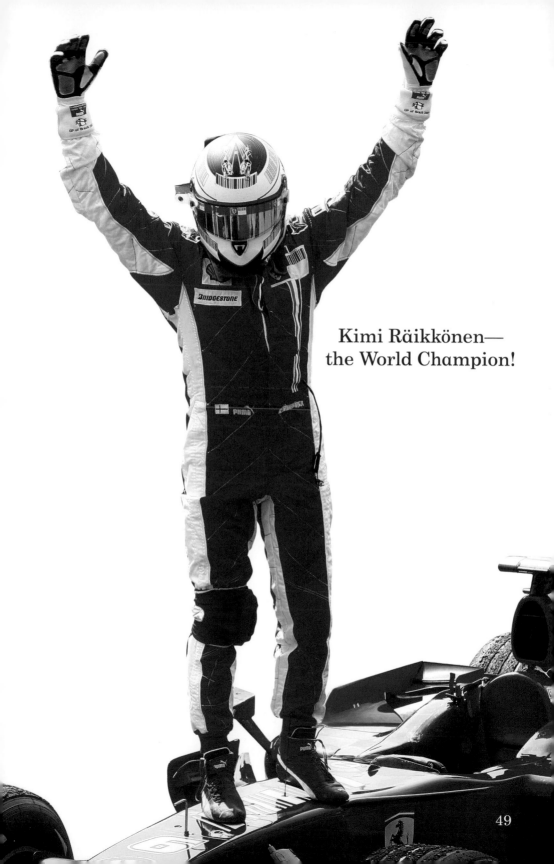

Kimi Räikkönen—
the World Champion!

Activities

The activities at the back of this book help you to practice the following skills:

✏️ Spelling and writing

📖 Reading

💬 Speaking

🎧 Listening

❓ Critical thinking

✿ Preparation for the Cambridge Young Learners exams

1 **Choose the correct answers, and write the full sentences in your notebook.** 📖 ✏️ ⭐

1 Scuderia Ferrari is one of the great names in . . . racing.
   a bike   **b** horse
   c motor   **d** motorbike

2 In 1929, Enzo started his own . . . called Scuderia Ferrari.
   a team   **b** pair
   c group   **d** band

3 The first of Scuderia Ferrari's many . . . came in the Mille Miglia race.
   a competitions **b** games
   c jobs   **d** victories

2 **In your notebook, write a news story about the 1948 Mille Miglia.** ✏️ ❓

THE MILLE MIGLIA

Yesterday, Scuderia Ferrari won the Mille Miglia race!

3 **Listen to Chapter Two. In your notebook, describe what's happening.** 🎧* ✏️

The next great victory for Scuderia Ferrari was . . .

4 **You are José Froilán González. Ask and answer questions with a friend, using the words in the box.** 💬

Formula 1 Grand Prix   in front
Drivers' World Championships
first success   Silverstone

1

Which is the most exciting motor race in the world?

It's the Formula 1 Grand Prix!

2 Where did you race in it?

3 Who was the favorite to win, and why?

4 Where was he at the beginning of the race?

5 What did the victory mean for Scuderia Ferrari?

5 **Read Chapter Three. Are sentences 1—5 *True* or *False*? If there is not enough information, write *Doesn't say*. Write the answers in your notebook.** 📖 ✏️

1 There are two drivers in one car in the 24 Hours of Daytona race in the USA.

2 The American Ford team was the favorite to win the race in 1967.

3 The American Ford team had six cars and 200 people to work on them.

4 Scuderia Ferrari had only two cars and fifteen people to work on them.

6 **Write sentences using *After*, *As*, *But*, or *so* in your notebook.** 📖 ✏️

1 . . . the hours passed, the Fords stopped one after the other.

2 . . . the 330 P4s just drove and drove.

3 . . . a drive of 4,083 kilometers, Bandini and Amon won.

4 The other two Ferrari cars came second and third, . . . they drove around the racetrack together to celebrate Ferrari's amazing victory.

7 **Read the definitions from Chapter Four.**
Write the correct words in your notebook.

1 a competition to find the best car
maker in Formula 1 **c . . .**

2 where you are in a race or competition,
for example, first, second, last **p . . .**

3 a road or path in a race that goes
around to end where it starts **l . . .**

4 to move more slowly **s . . .**

5 the winner of a race, game,
or competition **c . . .**

8 **Write complete sentences in your notebook,**
using *Regazzoni* or *Lauda*.

1 In 1975, Ferrari's top driver, . . . , wanted to
win the Drivers' World Championship.

2 Ferrari's other driver, . . . , had the fastest
start and was in first place for the whole race.

3 At lap 40, . . . had a problem with his car, so he
slowed down.

4 . . . was third, which was enough for him to
become World Champion.

9 **Match the two parts of the sentences.
Write the full sentences in your notebook.**

1 At the Monaco Grand Prix,

2 Everyone said that the Ferraris couldn't win

3 A turbo engine is very good for driving fast

> **a** because they had turbo engines.
>
> **b** but not good for turning slowly.
>
> **c** the cars race through the streets of the city of Monte Carlo.

10 **Write the sentences in the correct order.**

Then, on lap 53 of 76 laps, Piquet drove off the racetrack.

Gilles Villeneuve, in the first Ferrari, was a long way behind the leading teams' drivers.

On lap 72, Villeneuve passed Jones and won the race.

Then, Jones had a problem with his car, and he slowed down.

11 **Listen to Chapter Six. Answer the questions below in your notebook.** 🎧* 📖 ✏️

1 When was the San Marino Grand Prix?

2 How many new drivers did Scuderia Ferrari have?

3 Where was Gilles Villeneuve from?

4 How did Villeneuve die?

5 When did Villeneuve die?

12 **Read the answers, and write the questions in your notebook.** 📖 ✏️ ❓

1 The race was between Tambay and Patrese.

2 With only five laps to go, Patrese drove off the racetrack.

3 Tambay won and Arnoux came third.

4 Tambay waved the Canadian flag at the end of the race.

5 To celebrate and remember Villeneuve.

13 **Choose the correct words, and write the full sentences in your notebook.** 📖 ✏️

1 On August 14th 1988, Enzo Ferrari **died / was dying** in Italy.

2 The Italian Grand Prix **happened / was happening** a month later at Monza.

3 Scuderia Ferrari **didn't have / weren't having** much hope for the race. At that time, the McLaren team **won / were winning** everything!

4 The two Ferrari drivers, Berger and Alboreto, **came / were coming** first and second.

5 The newspapers **wrote, / were writing,** "Someone up there loves you, Ferrari!" They **thought / were thinking** about Enzo Ferrari.

14 **Talk to a friend about Enzo Ferrari. Ask and answer questions.** 💬

When was Enzo Ferrari born?

Enzo Ferrari was born in 1898.

15 Choose the correct words, and write the full sentences in your notebook.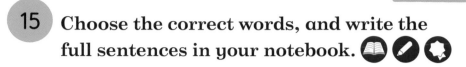

1	Constructors' Championship	Drivers' World Championship	Grand Prix
2	amazing	car	driver
3	Champion	Place	Success

1 In 1979, Jody Scheckter won the . . . in a Ferrari. After that, there was a long wait for Ferrari fans.

2 But in 2000, a young German . . . , Michael Schumacher, was close to changing that for Scuderia Ferrari.

3 If he won the Japanese Grand Prix at Suzuka, he would be the World . . .

16 Write a letter from Michael Schumacher to his mother at the end of Chapter Eight.

Hi Mom,
You won't believe what happened to me today . . .

17 Read the text below. Find the five mistakes, and write the correct text in your notebook.

Juan Manuel Fangio won seven Drivers' World Championships between 1951 and 1957. In 2002, Michael Schumacher won it for the sixth time.

The final Grand Prix of 2003 was at Suzuka, Korea. Fangio needed to finish in eighth place or higher to win the race.

18 Describe Michael Schumacher in your own words in your notebook.

Michael Schumacher is a famous racing driver. He . . .

19 **Complete the sentences in your notebook, using words from Chapter Ten.** 📖 ✏️ 🏁

1 When Kimi Räikkönen, driving for Ferrari, started the last race of the year in Brazil, . . .

2 He was seven points . . .

3 To win the Championship, Räikkönen needed to win the race, and Hamilton . . .

4 When the race started, Felipe Massa's and Räikkönen's Ferraris raced in front, and . . .

20 **Read the text, and write all the text with the correct verbs in your notebook.** 📖 ✏️

Massa . . . (**be**) in front, with Räikkönen just behind him. Then, the two Ferraris quickly . . . (**change**) places, and Räikkönen . . . (**win**)!

But where . . . (**be**) Hamilton? He only . . . (**finish**) in seventh place so Kimi Räikkönen . . . (**win**) the Drivers' World Championship!

It . . . (**be**) another success for Ferrari in a long line of victories—and there . . . (**be**) sure to . . . (**be**) many more of them in the future!

Projects

21 In this book, you read about these racing drivers from the past.

Niki
Lauda

Gilles
Villeneuve

Michael
Schumacher

Find out about another Ferrari racing driver now. Work in a group to make a presentation about them. Include the information below:

- What is the racing driver called?

- Where are they from?

- What competitions have they won?

- What do you like about them?

Projects

22 **Look online, and find out five interesting things about Scuderia Ferrari.**

Talk to a friend. Say five things about Scuderia Ferrari that are true, and five things that are not true.

Ask your friend to guess which things are true.

Then, listen to your friend, and guess which of the things they say are true.

Glossary

amazing *(adjective)*
Something that makes
you feel surprised and
happy is *amazing*.

celebrate *(verb)*
to do something to
remember something
or someone

champion *(noun)*
the winner of a race,
game, or competition

championship *(noun)*
a competition to find
the best of something

**Constructors'
Championship** *(noun)*
a competition to find
the best car maker in
Formula 1

**Drivers' World
Championship** *(noun)*
a competition to find the
best driver in Formula 1

Formula 1 *(noun)*
a kind of racing with
very fast cars

Grand Prix *(noun)*
a race in Formula 1

lap *(noun)*
a road or path in a race
that goes around to end
where it starts

motor racing *(noun)*
a sport. Cars race in
motor racing.

place *(noun)*
where you are in a
race or competition,
for example, first,
second, last

racetrack *(noun)*
a road that is used
for races

slow down *(verb)*
to move more slowly

success *(noun)*
when you do well and
get what you wanted

tire *(noun)*
something on the outside
of a wheel, usually filled
with air

turbo *(short for
turbocharger) (noun)*
a kind of engine

victory *(noun)*
when you win in
a game, race, or fight

Visit **www.ladybirdeducation.co.uk**
to choose your next book!